W9-ALN-137

DINO-THANKSGIVING

LISA WHEELER
ILLUSTRATIONS BY BARRY GOTT

CAROLRHODA BOOKS · MINNEAPOLIS

For all the grandparents who've made Thanksgiving
memorable. You know who you are! —L.W.

For Rose, Finn, and Nandi —B.G.

Carolrhoda Books®
An imprint of Lerner Publishing Group, Inc.
241 First Avenue North
Minneapolis, MN 55401 USA

For reading levels and more information, look up this title at
www.lernerbooks.com.

Additional images of leaves by enjoynz/Getty Images, paprika/Shutterstock.com.

Designed by Kimberly Morales.
Main body text set in Churchward Samoa. Typeface provided by Chank.
The illustrations in this book were created in Adobe Illustrator, Photoshop,
and Corel Painter.

Library of Congress Cataloging-in-Publication Data

Names: Wheeler, Lisa, 1963– author. | Gott, Barry, illustrator.
Title: Dino-Thanksgiving / Lisa Wheeler ; illustrations by Barry Gott.
Description: Minneapolis : Carolrhoda Books®, [2020] | Series: Dino-holidays
  | Audience: Ages 5–9. | Audience: Grades 2–3. | Summary: The dinosaurs
  enjoy a variety of Thanksgiving Day activities, including preparing favorite
  recipes, playing touch football, telling stories, and eating together.
Identifiers: LCCN 2019049721 (print) | LCCN 2019049722 (ebook) |
  ISBN 9781512403183 (library binding) | ISBN 9781541599383 (ebook)
Subjects: CYAC: Stories in rhyme. | Dinosaurs—Fiction. | Thanksgiving Day—
  Fiction.
Classification: LCC PZ8.3.W5668 Djj 2020 (print) | LCC PZ8.3.W5668
  (ebook) | DDC [E]—dc23

LC record available at https://lccn.loc.gov/2019049721
LC ebook record available at https://lccn.loc.gov/2019049722

Manufactured in the United States of America
1-39169-21083-2/11/2020

In autumn, there's a thankful mood—
a holiday that's filled with food.

All the dinos jump and squeal.
Thanksgiving! It's their favorite meal.

DINO-MART

12 ITEMS OR FEWER

Every dino-airport's slammed.
Every road and highway jammed.

Arrivals		Departures	
PALEODELPHIA	07:45	PANGEVELAND	07:33
CRETACECAGO	08:11	JURASSICSONVILLE	08:00
MESOZOPOLIS	08:26	TRIASSICOMA	08:46
DES MIOCENES	09:02	LOS GONDWANGELES	09:33
CENOLUMBUS	09:36	LEMURISTON	10:14
NEW ORINTHLEANS	10:06	PERMIANAPOLIS	CANCELLED

GATE 7

DASA

No matter where each dino roams,
today, there is no place like home.

T. rex wakes at crack of dawn.

It's time to put the turkey on.

He takes the bird out of the brine,

seasons it with sage and thyme.

DINO SUGAR

Although it won't be done till five,
by noon his guests will all arrive!

Compy eyes the roasting meat.
"I'm hungry! Is it time to eat?"

The TV's on at **Troodon's**.

They watch as dinos twirl batons.

The gleaming floats are all displayed.

It's the Dino-Thanksgiving Parade!

Balloons go by as **Minmi** cheers.

She went to see it live this year!

As drummers drum and trumpets blare,

a giant turkey floats in air.

Tricera sautés greens with ease,
using Grandma's recipes.

He mixes nuts into a bowl
for sweet potato casserole.

The broccoli's chopped. The salad's tossed.
He's boiling up cranberry sauce.

There's corn and beans and fruit galore—
no turkey for this veggiesaur!

Some dinos leave their neighborhoods,
go over the river and through the woods.

Allo follows Stego's gaze.

"Let's get lost inside a maze!"

The dinosaurs decide to race.
Between the rows, Leso gives chase.

Compy's time cannot be beat.
"I'm hungry! Is it time to eat?"

As crawling babies scatter toys,
the football game is background noise.

The **Pteros** watch. It's twin and twin.
Both brothers hope the **Redscales** win.

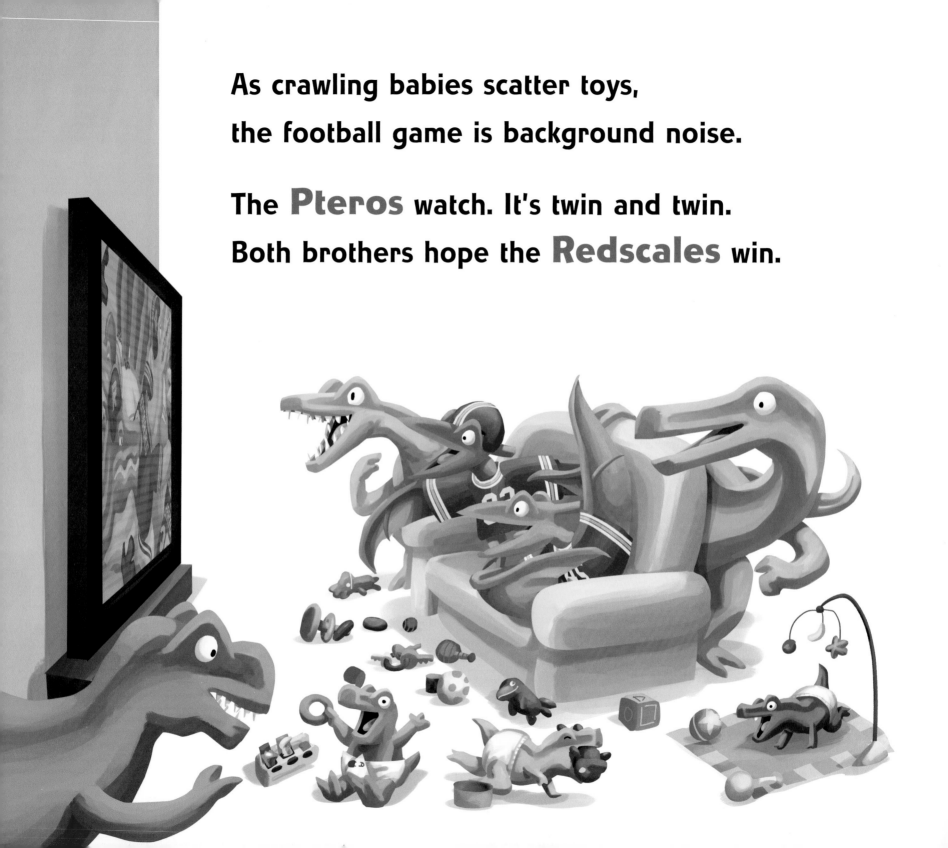

Next door, amidst the pots and pans,
the house is full of **Snacker** fans.

As football lovers cheer and shout,
dino-kids run in and out.

Out back, little cousins play:
Ping-pong, tag, and lawn croquet.

Raptor helps them fly a kite.
They're building up an appetite!

The children won't be underfoot.
(Although their kite has gone caput!)

Compy rolls up on the street.

"I'm hungry! Is it time to eat?"

Inside, dinner cooks and steams.
Outside, dinos pick their teams.

Flag football is an old tradition.
It keeps the rowdies from the kitchen.

Playing is a lot of fun.

Watch the dinos pass and run.

No time to find out which team won . . .

"Dinner's done!"

Compy is the first one in.

He wipes the drool off of his chin.

There's turkey, stuffing, pie, and more!

They all share what they're thankful for.

"Football!"

"Friends!"

"A winning team!"

"Mom and Dad!"

"My twin!"

"Ice cream!"

Over at **Tricera's** place,
smiles appear on every face.

Each one brought a dish to share:
fruit and veggies everywhere!

They all join hands—from large to least.

They're truly thankful for this feast.

Then . . .

Uncles boast and aunties chatter.
Pets upset the turkey platter!

That chair doesn't look too stable.
Food fights at the kiddie table!

Old stories told, some dinos weep,
then Gram and Grandpa fall asleep.

When each scrumptious dish is passed
and the meal is done at last,

some dinos sit and sip a cup
while others start the washing up.

Then all the dinos come together
in crisp and chilly autumn weather.

They walk, to calm their tummies down,
to a bonfire at the edge of town.

They played. They laughed.
They worked. They ate.
All agree this day was great.

They look ahead to warmer days . . .

. . . when Dino-Easter's on its way!